BLO

Blocksma, Mary

The best dressed
bear

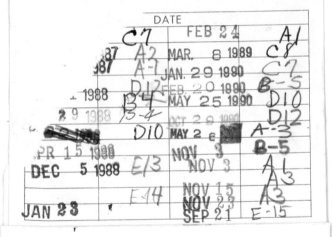

DATE		
C7	FEB 24	A1
A2	MAR. 8 1989	C8
A-7	JAN. 29 1990	C7
D12	FEB. 20 1990	B-5
B4	MAY 25 1990	D10
B-4	OCT 29 1990	D12
D10	MAY 2	A-3
	NOV 3	B-5
E/3	NOV 3	A1
	NOV 15	A3
E14	NOV 23	A3
	SEP 21	E-15

87
987
1988
29 1988
PR 15 1988
DEC 5 1988
JAN 23

A JUST ONE MORE BOOK
Just For You

The Best Dressed Bear

by Mary Blocksma

Illustrated by Sandra Cox Kalthoff

Developed by The Hampton-Brown Company, Inc.

 CHILDRENS PRESS™

CHICAGO

Word List

Give children books they can read by themselves, and they'll always ask for **JUST ONE MORE**. This book is written with 80 of the most basic words in our language, all repeated in an appealing rhythm and rhyme.

a	everyone	left	pair	tie
am		like	pants	to
and	for	look		town
at	fox		said	two
		me	sale	
back	goat	more	see	wear
be	go(ing)		sheep	went
bear	get	need(s)	shirt	what
best	got	new	shoe(s)	when
but		not	so	with
	hat	now	socks	wonderful
can(not)	he		something	wow
cat	how	of	store	
coat	I('m)	off		yet
come	in	oh	tail	you
	it	on	that	
dance		one	the	
door	just	or	then	
down		out	there('s)	
dressed	kangaroo		thing	
			this	

Library of Congress Cataloging in Publication Data

Blocksma, Mary.
  The best dressed bear.

  (Just one more)
  Summary: A bear who wishes to be the best dressed bear at a dance receives help from all the animal clerks in the store.
    1. Children's stories, American. [1. Bears—Fiction. 2. Animals—Fiction. 3. Clothing and dress—Fiction] I. Kalthoff, Sandra Cox, ill. II. Title. III. Series.
PZ7.B6198Be 1984   [E]   84-9565
ISBN 0-516-01585-0   AACR2

A bear went down to a store in town.

"A dance!" said the bear.
"I am going to a dance!
WHAT can I wear
to be the best dressed bear?"

"Socks!" said the fox.

"Get socks that are new.

You can get one.

Or, you can get two."

"New socks!" said the bear.
"Just LOOK at me. Wow!
I am the best dressed bear—
AND HOW!"

"Not yet! Get a shoe!"
said the kangaroo.
"You can get one.
Or, you can get two!"

"New shoes!" said the bear.
"Just LOOK at me. Wow!
I AM the best dressed bear—
AND HOW!"

"Not yet," said the sheep.
"You need to wear
a shirt and a tie
to be a best dressed bear."

"A shirt and a tie,"
said the bear. "Oh, wow!
Now I am the best dressed bear—
AND HOW!"

"Not yet!" said the goat.
"Get a coat with a tail.
Look at this coat!
You can get it on sale."

"A coat with a tail!"
said the bear. "Oh, wow!
"Now I am the best dressed bear—
AND HOW!"

"Not yet!" said the cat.
"You need a new hat.
You cannot go
in a hat like THAT!"

"A hat!" said the bear.
"Just look at me. Wow!
Now I'm the best dressed bear—
AND HOW!"

"I'm the best," said the bear.
"I'm the best I can be."

"I'm off to the dance
so EVERYONE can see!"

Then the bear left
to go out the door.
But everyone said,
"There's JUST ONE MORE!"

"There's one more thing
you need for the dance.
Bear, you need
a pair of . . ."

"Pants!" said the bear
when he got to the door.

"A BEST dressed bear
needs something more."

So he went to the dance
in a new pair of pants.

And EVERYONE said,

when the bear got there . . .

"Look!" said the bear.
"Just look at me now!"

"Now I AM
the best dressed bear."